EXHIBITION TEXT

For Josephine

Acknowledgements: Excerpt by Michael Benedikt, from *For An Architecture of Reality*, copyright ©1987 by Michael Benedikt. Reprinted by permission of the author; Excerpt by Anne Carson, from *NOX*, copyright ©2010 by Anne Carson. Reprinted by permission of New Directions Publishing Corp; Excerpt by Moyra Davey, from *INDEX CARDS*, ©2020 by Moyra Davey. Reprinted by permission of New Directions Publishing Corp; *Index Cards*, Moyra Davey. London, Fitzcarraldo Editions, 2020. Copyright © Moyra Davey, 2020; Excerpt by John Kelsey, from *Rich Texts*, ©2010 by John Kelsey. Reprinted by permission of Sternberg Press and Institut für Kunstkritik.

First published 2024 by Vagabond Press
www.vagabondpress.net

© D. Frederick Thomas 2024

Cover image used under license from Shutterstock.com.

ISBN 978-1-925735-73-4

This project has been assisted by the Australian Government through Creative Australia, its principal arts investment and advisory body.

Australian Government

D. FREDERICK THOMAS
EXHIBITION TEXT

VAGABOND PRESS

How does one part of reality, art, come to be regarded as being characteristically about the rest?

Michael Benedikt, *For An Architecture of Reality*

Sometimes, we wonder if it even matters what we say when we write about art, so why not write about saying nothing instead?

John Kelsey, *Rich Texts: Selected Writings for Art*

'Overtakelessness' is a word told me by a philosopher once: *das Unumgängliche* – that which cannot be got round. Cannot be avoided or seen to the back of. And about which one collects facts – it remains beyond them.

Anne Carson, *Nox*

1.

On the 19th of February, 2022, my friend S____, an artist, asked if I would be interested in writing the exhibition text for her contribution to a group show she'd been invited to take part in later in the year. "I completely understand if you want to say no," she said. I told her I'd think about it but that I absolutely wanted to. I asked when the show was. "October," she said. The conversation actually unfolded over the course of a time delay and in text messages, not spoken, as might be implied by the way I've just written it out. S____, at the time, was living outside of Baltimore, Maryland and I was living in Brisbane, Australia. Her initial question, whether I would be interested, and the additional assurance that I could say no if I wanted to, both arrived in the middle of the night for me, and I found them waiting on the lock screen of my phone when I woke up. I replied as I waited for the kettle to boil so I could make my coffee. My additional question, about when the exhibition actually was, I sent later in the morning, after a second cup of coffee and after I'd kissed J_____ goodbye outside our apartment as she headed off for work and I set off for a walk to the library to pick up some books that I had reserved and that were waiting for me after a slight delay during which I presumed I'd had to wait for someone else to return them, a series of short novels by a British novelist all of which formed a kind of extended meditation on the way class informed consciousness, though not—the novels—in a polemical sort of way, just working around the edges of the idea in the way that good novels sometimes do. Though at the time I didn't know whether or not the novels actually succeeded; I'd simply listened to an interview with the author and decided to request the books right then, before I'd even heard the end of the interview. I'd read something else by her, years before, and remembered it being quite engrossing, so I was looking forward to immersing myself once again in her consciousness. But I sent the second text, asking when the exhibition actually was, while walking, typing it out a bit inarticulately as I half-focused on my progress down the sidewalk, having to correct a couple mistypings before hitting send. S_____'s response came immediately, since by that time we were both awake in our separate time zones on either side of the planet, she in her evening, me in my morning. And I'd then responded immediately in kind and said, "In Baltimore?" And she'd asked if she should just call me, at which point I'd explained, still in text, that I was out walking and was almost to the library, but that I could call her once I'd gotten my books and was walking back, since I wouldn't have to cut the call short at that point, could just keep talking once I got home, maybe have a cup of tea and sit out on the deck if we got deep into conversation. "That sounds good," she said. "I'll call in fifteen minutes, at most," I typed back. Then I put my phone in my pocket and walked the last block or two to the library, a small local branch that was basically the size of a double-wide trailer, with rickety wooden steps up to a small wooden porch outside the sliding door and an equally rickety wheelchair ramp to the right of the steps, doglegging its way away from and back towards the porch. Inside, the computers were all occupied, in the children's section one of the librarians was leading a story time for infants and their mothers. I went over to where the reserves were shelved and found the books I was there to pick up, carried them to the automatic checkout station and scanned them one by one, waiting for the little green check marks to appear on the screen, then I went back outside and paused at the bottom of the steps to pull my phone back out of my pocket so I could call S_____. It rang a few times and then stopped. I'd started walking again, holding the phone to my ear as I strolled back along the way I'd come, the books in my other hand—I didn't stop walking but slowed down as I glanced at my screen to make sure she hadn't picked up and I just wasn't hearing her because of a connection issue. The call had ended though. I stopped walking and texted her quickly to let her know I'd called. "Yeah. Sorry. Just needed to pee. One sec," she texted back. "You could have answered and just not told me," I responded. "Yeah, but it would have felt dishonest," she texted. Then my screen showed that she was calling so I answered and started walking again, greeting her by immediately asking, "So how is this any less awkward than if you'd just answered in the first place and told me you were peeing?" "The fact that we texted about it softened the blow," she said. I could hear her smiling. "Good pee?" I asked conversationally. "Very good pee," she said before asking what books I'd been picking up from the library. I told her the name of the author and the titles of the books but none of it rang a bell for her. I told her I'd let her know if they were worth her time, if they seemed like the kind of thing she'd be interested in, then we started talking about the group show she'd texted me about overnight. It turned out it was actually going to be in Boston, at an art space she'd never been to but that some friends of hers had founded a year earlier and was doing really well. Other mutual friends had been invited to do a show there and she had been invited to take part. Every artist was encouraged to source their own text or texts from whoever they thought would best be able to respond to their work. S____ said I'd been the first person she'd thought of, without even having to consider the question. I felt myself blushing and told her I was flattered. "Like I said, I completely understand if you want to say no," she said. "I *want* to say yes," I said, before adding, "I just feel like—can you send me photos of the work? How can I write about it from all the way over here? Is it painting? Photography? Sculpture? Something else?" S____ was fairly wide-ranging in the kind of work she made, and we didn't actually tend to talk about what we were each working on at any given time, so I didn't really know what she'd been up to recently, nor did she know what I'd been doing, in terms of my writing. "It's not really photographable," she said, sounding thoughtful. She said, "You're right that the geography makes it difficult. I wondered if maybe you'd be interested in coming here sometime in the next few months." "To Baltimore?" I asked. "Yeah, you could stay with me and spend time with the work, write whatever came to you, then head back to your Antipodean wonderland." I laughed and said, "I don't think I could afford it. The flight, I mean." "I'd pay," she said without a moment's hesitation. I frowned. "Could *you* afford it?" I asked. "My day job gave everyone big holiday bonus gift cards instead of paying actual reasonable wages throughout the year so I've got this weird internet money sitting in my inbox. I think I can use that." "Are you sure?" I asked. "I'll double check," she said, "but if I can, then yes. You'd be into that idea if the money worked out?" "Probably, yes," I said. "I'll look into it tomorrow and let you know." We talked for a minute or two longer before hanging up just as I got home. While I waited for the kettle to boil, I texted J_____ a basic summary of S_____'s proposal. She responded and said it sounded like a great idea. "You can visit your parents while you're over there," she texted. "It's true," I replied. They were getting old. "I think you should do it," she texted. "Okay, good," I texted back. "Do you WANT to do it?" she texted. "I think so," I replied. "We can talk later," she texted, before adding, "I've got a meeting in a minute." "Have a good meeting," I texted. "I will," she replied. I set my phone down and took my coffee out on to the deck. I was carrying the pile of library books around like a little kid carrying around new toys on Christmas day, just kind of enjoying the tactile pleasure of a stack of books and what they suggested, the kind of potential suggested by their physical presence on the table. I glanced at the back cover of the first book in the series then put it back on the pile, not in the mood to actually read right then. I sipped my coffee and tried to decide whether I actually felt capable of writing S_____'s exhibition text. That was the real sticking point. It would be wonderful to see her, and J_____ was right that I could visit my parents in New York while I was in the same country as them, but the question was whether I felt capable of the actual writing, especially not really knowing what I'd be writing about. But there was something deeply appealing about that kind of complete uncertainty. It would be a challenge. And I trusted S____. If I had been the first person she'd thought of to write about whatever she'd been working on, it meant that she was open to whatever I would come up with, that she was more interested in putting my consciousness into conversation with whatever her consciousness had produced and wanted to use whatever my consciousness then generated as a way to contextualize whatever it was her consciousness had produced. The job of a written response to a work of art in a show, in a sense, was to provide a model for someone uncertain of how to interact with the artwork, to show them how another mind had found a way in, to draw a kind of sketched map of an unfamiliar terrain. Even if the map barely corresponded to what they themselves were seeing with their own eyes, there in front of them, what mattered was the fact that someone else had been there first, had left a mark. It was to perform a gaze and document that gaze, to instruct others as to *how* to gaze, or how one might consider gazing, even if they subsequently chose to gaze in another way entirely. Wasn't that what *all* writing did? In that sense, was there anything any more daunting about what S____ was asking me to do than what I already did regularly and had done countless times in the past? To record my own consciousness as it tried to make sense of something new? I finished my coffee, picked the books back up and went inside.

2.

One month later, I flew to Baltimore, first going non-stop from Brisbane to Los Angeles then catching a domestic flight from LAX to JFK and then another flight down from New York to Baltimore. I spent the entire 13 hour flight across the Pacific reading a bunch of stuff that S_____ had emailed to me to give an idea of the kind of thing she was thinking might be useful for me to have in mind when I arrived. It was a strange combination of texts, a kind of .pdf library that she'd sent to me as a single zipped folder; I'd printed it all out so I could just read it without worrying about my battery dying or some download issue making it so that suddenly I wouldn't be able to access one thing or another on the plane. I liked paper anyway, there was something sturdy about it, something contained and limited, the writing and the thinking it expressed ended at the edges of the page, instead of there being a strange sense of the screen as a window into something that continued unseen beyond the borders, never within reach. I liked making notes on paper too. I had a pencil in hand and wrote in the margins the whole time, sleeping a bit during the flight but mostly reading and writing my thoughts as I went, pausing to eat, occasionally pausing to watch some of a single movie that I kept going back to. The first .pdf—I'd arranged them in a stack in the same order they'd been in in the zipped folder—was an interview with an architect about a theory he'd developed and spent his entire life trying to turn into an actual physical practice, which seemed to be all about designing buildings that would somehow appear to their occupants to be proportionately larger inside as the number of occupants increased, and conversely appear to be smaller as the number of occupants decreased. Though he had also experimented with the inverse, designing spaces that would appear larger the emptier they were, and not just as a function of there being less people in them but in a way that would amplify that decrease in occupancy, and he had also experimented with designing spaces that would create a kind of claustrophobia even in someone not otherwise inclined to feeling claustrophobic, spaces that would seem to literally shrink at an accelerated rate as the number of people within them increased. There was a bit of detail about how these effects were achieved but it didn't really make sense to me, and it also wasn't entirely clear from the interview whether the architect had ever actually successfully created any of these spaces or whether it had all remained in the realm of theory. The interview had been published in 1975 and the .pdf was a scanned copy, the folds in the paper recreated in the images of the pages, the slight curve of the text at the sides where the magazine had been pressed open into the scanner. I finished reading and moved onto the next thing, which I recognized immediately as Duchamp's notes for his final work, *Étant donnés*. I'd read them before but took my time turning the pages, revisiting it all as part of the sequence of ideas that S____ had sent my way. By that point the plane had been in the air for an hour or two, including that strange period after takeoff and before the plane reaches the altitude at which it tends to stay for most of the trip, the initial period during which one is constantly made aware of one's environment ascending or rotating to one side or another along an axis, a feeling in the pit of the stomach with nothing external to corroborate or contextualize the feeling. Reading slowly, I had paused during those moments, as I always did, not out of a sense of anxiety but more out of a sense of presence, of a desire not to simply become inured to my own reality within whatever moment or sequence of moments I happened to find myself at any given time. I didn't fly often, especially back from Australia to America, and the experience was always a little more dissociative then I expected it to be while simultaneously feeling less profound than I often thought it should feel, traversing the globe with such relative speed. But it wasn't the traversing or the speed that made me feel a sense of dissociation, it was something else. I supposed if I'd been able to put it into words, it wouldn't have persisted. Or that was my writer's fantasy, at least. I imagined those who made visual art probably had similar experiences often enough, and then made paintings or sculptures or took photographs or did whatever it was they did, and never quite managed to articulate whatever it was they'd felt or perceived. Success wasn't useful. Success just shut down forward momentum. Better to always be grasping at something just a little out of reach, artistic practice as a way to kind of wilfully put oneself back into a childlike place of perpetual frustration and yearning. No wonder Duchamp had gone and taken a break to play chess for two decades, not that that was what he'd actually done. Had that final work of his been made in a state of trying to stave off, for as long as possible, that experience of failure, of not having quite succeeded? Or had he been, rather, so certain that he would finally have succeeded once he completed it—and this would then, too, be why he hadn't made the work public until after his death, since a work of art wasn't really complete until it had been made so in the eyes of an audience, even if that audience was just an audience of one, and I never imagined that he thought of his wife, who worked with him on *Étant donnés*, as such an audience, as particularly distinct from him—that he took his time, made the final work, and died finally free of that nagging sense of inconclusiveness? The movie I watched—the first half hour after reading the Duchamp notes, the rest later on after more reading—was a superhero movie about a young man who developed the ability to step through time but in a literal way, taking steps forward or backward and advancing time as he did so, in the way that I supposed we all did when we stepped forward or backward, though a backward step for us, in real life, still corresponded to a movement forward in time, and this was what the film basically said, too, which was that his superpower was only useful for backwards travel, because a backwards step only moved time backwards by an interval equal to the amount of time it would take one to take a single step backwards. His forward steps, while operating on a superpowered level, were indistinguishable from anyone else's steps forward. He took a step forward and time moved forward. But when he stepped backward, time reversed, so that the first major action sequence of the film unfolded as a strange sort of backwards stumbling run towards confused foes who seemed always to be just about to throw a punch or draw a gun or knife on the protagonist of the film, but each ungainly lurch he took backwards caused time to skitter backwards, halting his enemies' movements, arresting them in time and making them move just the littlest bit in reverse, buying him enough of an advantage each time to throw a punch of his own, or dodge out of the way, and then as he encountered one foe near the end of the sequence there was a moment when he finally seemed to realize the extent of what his power enabled him to do, and he took a deep breath and committed to a strange kind of reverse-charge, moving straight past the foe who was trying to harm him so that suddenly the foe not only re-holstered his weapon but began to move backwards as well, a little behind the protagonist, or ahead of the protagonist, since the protagonist was moving in one direction while facing in the opposite direction so that he was able—and thus so were we, the viewing audience, over his shoulder, from his perspective—able to witness the no-longer-threatening foe walking backwards in the same direction as the backwards-running protagonist and then turning and moving backwards through an emergency exit into a stairwell from which he had clearly come earlier, making his way up into the building to the place where the protagonist had been ambushed, and then the door shut and the foe was entirely out of the picture, and the protagonist slowed his backward momentum, dealt with one final near-attack that he almost didn't notice coming—almost didn't move backwards fast enough to reverse—with a suddenly more confident backwards-moving punch, and then slowed to a halt, looking around to discover that he had survived, and then he turned around and fled the scene without going backwards anymore, simply hurrying to get away as quickly as possible. At which point I'd paused the movie and gone back to reading but the next text had been less easy for me to get my head around. Something about enamel. Something about the way a fingernail interacted with half-set enamel. I read it—it was only a few pages long—without retaining much of what I was reading, and then I closed my eyes for a bit. When I woke back up it was time for a meal to be served. The person sitting beside me was a man who looked like he was maybe in his sixties, with gray hair and narrow shoulders, he was thin and moved with a kind of lightness that made me like him immediately, as if the world was something he was walking on the surface of; he spoke with a slight lisp and smiled easily when he talked, but then listened, when he wasn't talking, with a kind of complete focus that caught me off guard at first but that I got used to after a minute or two. He was from Minnesota and had been visiting Australia to see a friend of his who had moved from the U.S. to Tasmania back in the nineties. They didn't see each other often, he and the friend, but tried to visit at least once a decade, and to make the visits significant, long enough to settle into. He'd been staying with his friend outside of Hobart for the last six weeks. The last time they'd seen each other, the friend had come back to the U.S. to visit my seatmate in Minneapolis. It had been winter and the friend had been away from the cold for long enough that my seatmate said he'd forgotten what it was like. Tasmania got cold enough in the winter, certainly, but not Minnesota cold. They'd spent the entire visit, more or less, sitting inside by the fire, reading books aloud to one another, listening to music, watching films, cooking, and only occasionally venturing out for walks when the temperature rose slightly higher than the punishingly low average. When the flight attendant came along the aisle with the drinks cart, my seatmate and I ordered the same thing, a glass of white wine each, and lingered over our drinks for a little while after finishing our food, chatting about this and that, before he downed his final sip, tucked the cup into the pouch on the back of the seat in front of him, and said that he was going to try to get some sleep. I said I might do the same, but first I'd try reading some more. He'd asked earlier, while we were eating, what it was I'd been reading and I'd sort of answered him, not so much with specific information about what I was reading so much as a general explanation as to why I was reading it. He wound up falling asleep and somehow staying asleep for most of the rest of the flight. I read a bit more, slept a bit, watched more of the movie, and kept rotating between those various ways of filling my time, along with another meal near the end of the flight, and then we landed. The final battle of the film culminated with the protagonist, the hero, discovering that if he stepped laterally in a particular way he could actually move time sideways, could shift over to a different version of events, a parallel moment informed by different decisions having been made before that moment, at which point, within that parallel moment, he could move forwards or backwards too, stepping laterally again to return to the version of reality that he was familiar with. Against all odds, overwhelmed by more foes than he could possibly hope to defeat by conventional means, even with his backwards running, he began to fight with a kind of wild leaping and stepping from one side to another, causing violent attackers to disappear and reappear elsewhere in the room, for example, or to no longer have weapons in their hands, and then, as he grew increasingly confident and took more and more steps in one direction to the right or the left, causing things to begin to change more dramatically, so that suddenly he found himself no longer in the room he'd been fighting in at all, but in a forest somewhere, a place he didn't know, and there was no one else there, just him alone, at peace, and he paused, breathing fast, still on edge, but then calmed himself and looked back to the left, as if trying to see where he'd come from, that other time, all those other times, and he couldn't, though he knew they were there, just a step away. And he suddenly saw, in flashback, his father, in a reprisal of a scene that had been central to the film's prologue, saying something to him about how we didn't choose our time, but the time we had was all about the choices we made, and after one last deep breath, his eyes closed and head tilted back, he cracked his neck, positioned himself as if in readiness to fight, and stepped back to the left. The rest of the fight was like a dance performance.

3.

S_____ was waiting for me at the airport when I got to Baltimore. It had been a while since we'd seen one another but I spotted her immediately in the midst of the other people gathered around outside the security gates, waiting to greet arriving passengers. She was tall and thin, with a big smile and high cheek bones, her dark hair cut short. She had taken the train to the airport so we walked back to where the platform was and waited for the next train back to the city. "It's so good to see you," she said. "You too," I said. I kept checking my phone to see if I had reception yet, connected to a different network, so I could let J_____ know I was alive, but I was still cut off. S_____ offered to send a message for me and I said that would be great. "Just let her know I'm here and I'll call once I have reception," I said. She held her phone up and took a photo of me before I realized what she was doing. "Photographic evidence," she said. The train pulled into the station and we got on along with a handful of other passengers, all of whom had more luggage than I did. We sat down and she finished texting J____ before putting her phone away. "So, did you read everything I sent you?" she asked. "I did," I said, which was true, since after the long flight there had been the rest of the trip across the U.S. As I'd gone on reading, the texts had seemed to get denser at a rate that seemed more accelerated than it would have had it just been a function of my increasing exhaustion, though my exhaustion had certainly increased dramatically as I'd neared the east coast—I realized suddenly, in fact, that I'd just drifted off next to S____ right there on the train and that she had asked a question about one of the texts she'd sent me to read on the plane, but also that J____ had responded to the message saying that I was alive and to the photo of me. I looked around, trying to gauge how much time had passed, but the view out the window was meaningless to me. "Sorry," I said, trying to wake myself up by opening my eyes as wide as possible. S____ laughed, clearly having been aware of my nodding off as it happened in front of her. "Don't worry about it. Just sleep. I'll wake you up when it's time to get off," she said. And I did exactly that, leaning against the window and closing my eyes. After what felt like a moment, S____ was shaking me awake. We got off the train. The night air was cold. We walked up a flight of stairs, out through a turnstile and across an echoic chamber with a mural along one of the walls then up another flight of steps and out onto a sidewalk. "My place is only a few blocks from here," she said. It was strange to be around one another again. The reality of it hit me only then, as we stepped out of the subway entrance and out into the open air, as if everything up to that point and since spotting her in the crowd of people outside the security gates had still belonged to the strange non-time of transit. Now I was here. Time resumed. I inhaled deeply and smelled the different air. S_____ naturally walked a step or two ahead of me. I didn't actually know what time it was. I tried to remember what time it had been when the plane had taken off, how long the last flight had been, what time we'd been scheduled to arrive, and then thought about how long we'd stood on the platform waiting for the train and how long the train ride had been. I'd fallen asleep. My phone wasn't telling the proper time yet. It felt late. The roads seemed empty. The train hadn't been very full, and then mostly with other people who had arrived on planes and taken the train into the city, other people with no proper sense of time. What did it matter anyway. We walked in silence for the couple blocks between the subway stop and S_____'s apartment building. When we got there, she let me in ahead of her and then led the way again up two flights of stairs to the third floor. The apartment was small and crowded with materials for making art. She lived alone. When we'd first met, years and years before, she'd been with a woman named M_____, but that relationship had ended during a long period of time in which we hadn't been in touch. I had stopped putting in any effort to maintain contact with S_____ and she hadn't put in any effort either and suddenly it had been five years since the last time we'd talked. We'd reconnected not long after that and been close again ever since, but I still carried a lot of guilt and shame about the way I'd let things slip. We'd never really talked about it, had just resumed things almost as if the five year gap had never happened, but I was constantly aware of a way in which I was never fully at ease, was always waiting for the moment when she would ask me what had happened, and despite having thought about it over and over throughout the years, both during the years in which we weren't talking and in the years since, I had trouble imagining what I would say. I felt like I was less a person than a thing always about to break into multiple pieces. On the phone, apart, in separate countries, it was easier to live with that feeling, so easy that it almost sometimes seemed as if it wasn't there, but as S_____ locked the door to her apartment behind me, I felt it as something not only no different than before, but as something almost possessing a weight, something tangible and frightening. It was as if a part of me suddenly believed that S_____'s entire reason for flying me here had been not to show me her work and elicit a response but to confront me finally about the way I had disappeared from her life like someone guilty of something. I had stopped talking to her during a difficult period in her life, when she and M_____ were falling apart, when M_____'s father, who had been like a father to her too, was dying of leukemia in hospice care in Florida and M_____ had been down there with him all the time and S_____ had been flying down on weekends both to be with M_____ and to be there for M_____'s father and to be there with M_____'s father for herself, and S_____ had been struggling to find a good reason to finish getting the Ph.D. she'd been pursuing for the better part of a decade but that no longer really mattered to her, yet she didn't want to work any kind of job other than the teaching jobs she would be eligible for once she completed her studies, and she hadn't been making art, she'd barely been sleeping, our conversations were all stilted, the last time we'd talked had been a strange conversation, a short call at an usual time of day for both of us, too early for her, too late for me, and suddenly, fifteen minutes in, she'd cut me off mid-sentence and said she didn't think she had it in her to keep talking, and I'd been caught off guard and said something like, "Yeah. I understand. I think I'm kind of in that head space too." And we'd hung up and not talked again for five years. I'd called occasionally but she'd never answered. I hadn't been sure I was dialing the right number. I'd emailed but she'd never responded save for once or twice, sending back short replies that never really went anywhere. And then things had resumed and now I was here, unsure of where in the apartment I was going to sleep. S_____ seemed to sense my confusion and apprehension. "Over here," she said, gesturing towards an alcove off the main living area which was lined with bookshelves; across the archway separating the alcove from the rest of the room she had run a curtain on a string between two nails. In the alcove was a mattress on the floor, though that makes it sound like it was a bare mattress when what it was was a made bed on the floor, just without a frame. It was a perfectly welcoming space and I immediately set my things down and sat down on the edge of the mattress. She told me where the bathroom was and asked if I needed anything or if I just wanted to sleep. "Just sleep," I said. "I'll see you in the morning," she said. She left the alcove's archway and turned off the lights in the main living room so that the only illumination was from the small lamp on a stool beside my bed. I turned off the lamp, took off my shoes in the dark as my eyes adjusted, then I lay down on top of the covers and immediately fell asleep.

4.

S_____'s studio wasn't in her apartment. The apartment was just a place where she kept things. It was as good a place as any. But the studio space was somewhere else, in another part of the city. She'd described it to me once, in an email, but I didn't really have a mental image of it, save for a vague recollection of her saying that it was in a building that she rented along with a dozen other artists and that her space in the building wasn't very big. I supposed, thinking about it, that trying to imagine any kind of artist's studio or writer's room was a strange exercise, since the place wasn't meaningful—the artist or writer was barely even meaningful. What mattered was the work that came out of the space, that came from the artist or writer. When I tried to picture S_____'s studio, I just wound up picturing works of hers that I'd seen over the years, whether in person or in reproductions, and then blending those different works together into a kind of room-shaped concept into the center of which I always placed S_____ as a kind of focal point. It was a mental image that never came fully into focus. In the morning, when I woke on the floor of the alcove, I felt as if I had crossed an invisible threshold into that unfocused image, or as if the image had settled over me like a mist or a sheet unfurled in the air above me as I slept, drifting down over me as if I was something to be covered. I sat up and looked around. The light in the alcove, filtering in through the window in the middle of the wall, was the gray winter light I remembered from my childhood, growing up not far from where I was now, a different city, different state, but same general part of the world. Time away had made me start to doubt whether it was how I remembered it. The night before hadn't changed that misapprehension, or apprehensive uncertainty—it had felt so unstable, so ill-defined, so half-awake. But the light now was clear, even as it peeked in around the lowered blinds, and when I stood and raised them and the light came in and lit the room properly, I let myself sink back down onto the mattress for a little while and just considered the way something like light was so different, the air it moved through, the things it fell on. I was a different person in one country than I was in another. S_____ had been right to bring me here. Even if the work *had* been photographable, it wouldn't have been the same work, not viewed in a different light. But if I was a different person, was I still the right person to respond to the work? What if what was required was the specific and impossible to attain alchemy of the version of my self that resided in Australia interacting with the version of the work that existed here, in Baltimore, over in S_____'s studio, and would remain relatively stable in the relatively similar context of Boston? But that was a question that felt utterly impossible to quantify, as I thought it through, there on the edge of the mattress on the floor; no one, or maybe only one or two people who would encounter the work and also bother to read whatever I wound up writing, would even know that the work and the writer were out of sync with one another. Maybe that was the point. I knew so little. I would have been out of sync no matter what. I stood up again and walked out of the alcove and down the hall to the bathroom where I peed and then splashed warm water on my face. S_____'s bedroom door was still shut—if she was awake she wasn't up yet. I went over to the kitchenette and filled the kettle with tap water to make coffee. I went over to the window and looked down at the street. It was too early for anyone to be heading to work yet. Back in the alcove, I heard my phone make a noise. I went to check it and saw that it had finally connected to a U.S. signal. I had 30 texts from J_____. The first one, from just before my flight had left Brisbane, said, 'Not sure if you've turned your phone off yet, but have a safe flight. I love you.' The last one, from five minutes ago, said, 'S_____ texted to say you were okay. Let me know when you have service. She sent a photo. You looked exhausted. Hope you got some sleep.' Just then the kettle started whistling back out on the stove. I stood to go turn it off and then heard S_____'s bedroom door open and her footsteps on the wood floor, then the kettle stopped whistling. I went out anyway, tucking my phone into my back pocket. "Sorry. My phone finally got service just now. I was making coffee. Did the sound wake you up?" I said. She was dressed but for all I knew she'd slept in her clothes. "No," she said, "I was up. I thought I heard you out here. Was just writing some stuff down. Did you sleep okay?" "Not long enough but that's to be expected after a long trip. I passed out immediately though," I said. "That's good. Do you want to just head over to the studio with me after you have your coffee? We can walk. Clear your head." "Is it far?" "Maybe a 20 minute walk." "That sounds good," I said. She had instant coffee on the counter. I heaped a spoonful into a chipped mug with a picture of a racecar on the side, poured hot water in, stirred and went to the fridge for milk. She went back to her bedroom for a few minutes while I drank my coffee. I pulled my phone out and texted J_____. 'Finally got a signal. Just having coffee then heading over to the studio,' I wrote. She texted back immediately: 'You got some sleep?' 'Enough to tide me over,' I wrote back. 'Are you nervous about seeing the work?' she texted. 'Too tired to be nervous,' I replied. 'That's probably ideal,' she texted. Then, in a second message, she added, 'Keep me posted.' 'I will,' I messaged her, before adding, 'Isn't it late there?' 'Not too late. I'm grading papers.' I finished my coffee and S_____ reappeared. I put my shoes and coat on and we headed out. The street was busier than it had been earlier when I'd looked out the window. S_____ was right about the morning air and the walk, within minutes I felt less foggy. By the time we got to the studio I felt less uncertain about everything. We went up to where her space was. The door was locked and we paused in the dark hallway while she fumbled with her keys. Then we went inside. My first impression of the space was that it was empty. It seemed like a room that hadn't been used in a long time, or had been used but not by someone like S_____, not an artist who made things, maybe by a performance artist, a dancer or something like that. My first impression didn't fade as my eyes adjusted to the low light—the room *was* empty. The one window had been covered with colorless fabric and only a little light got in around the edges. The floor was swept clean. The walls were unadorned. S_____ closed the door behind us and locked it behind her, then flicked a light switch and the fluorescent tube in the high ceiling flickered and popped to life above us. I blinked a few times against the glare of it and looked around again. "See," said S_____, "it's not really something I could photograph." "What is it?" I asked, because even as we stood for just a moment or two longer I became aware of something, even if I couldn't quite describe it to myself. The room wasn't *empty* so much as *not full*. Or maybe I was being overly generous, stepping too far across the line in order to try to meet something that just wasn't there to be met. But then she stepped further into the room and seemed to disappear. Not to slowly fade away or become obscured, not to drop out of sight or something like that. She was there and then she wasn't. I heard myself gasp aloud without even realizing I was doing it and then she reappeared just as suddenly, right in the same place she'd been when she'd vanished from sight. Then she disappeared again, only a couple yards away from me, maybe a third of the way into the small, artificially lit room with nothing in it save for us, or for me. "S_____!" I called out. And she came back again. She stood there, right at the place where I'd watched her seemingly wink in and out of existence twice in the span of no more than thirty seconds right in front of me, and I said, "How did you do that?" "Come see," she said, smiling. I stepped towards her, a little apprehensive but curious to understand what was actually taking place. And, quite suddenly—I felt as if I had lost complete control of my senses—the room snapped out from in front of me and turned into an entirely different room. I looked behind me and the room I'd just come from wasn't there anymore. Instead I was looking back at what it took me a moment to realize was a bedroom. I turned back around to look in the direction I'd walked, toward what had been the empty studio before it had suddenly changed, and saw a dresser against the wall to my right and a door in the middle of the far wall with a floor-to-ceiling mirror leaned against the wall beside it. The floor was mostly covered by a big, worn rug. There were clothes in a pile in front of the dresser. The door was closed. I turned back around again towards where I'd come from and realized part of what else had disoriented me when I'd looked back that way initially. There was a bed in one corner of the room, to my right. There wasn't a door though. I'd come, as far as I could tell, through the wall. Except the wall was farther away from me than where I'd come from; if I'd come *through the wall* then I wouldn't already be so far into the middle of the room. I turned around more so that I was facing a window I hadn't at first realized was there, in the middle of the wall that, as I'd followed S_____ and lost my sense of spatial orientation for a moment, would have been to my right. Now I was facing it and I walked over to it. I looked out and saw a view that confused me if only because of the route we'd taken up through the building to S_____'s studio space. I was looking down three stories to the street but, unless I had gotten more turned around than I'd realized, it was a street that was where the inside of the building should have been. I supposed it was a street that *was* where the inside of the building actually was. I turned back to face into the room just as the door opened and S____ came in carrying two glasses of water. She pushed the door shut behind her with her foot and crossed over to where I was still standing by the window. She handed me one of the glasses and she said, "So?" I looked back in the direction of the wall through which it seemed like I'd come and then at the door, then at the pile of clothes on the floor. I looked back at S____. She grinned. "Come through here," she said. "I can see you're not quite there yet," she added, walking towards the door through which she'd come with the glasses of water.

5.

"Is – is this... your apartment...?" I asked, as soon as we'd stepped through the door and into a hallway that I immediately recognized as the same hallway through which I'd entered S____'s apartment the night before, and through which we'd passed just a little while ago, that morning, leaving her apartment to walk over here to her studio. Or to her apartment, if that's where we were. It made no sense. I looked back toward the bedroom through the open door—she hadn't closed it behind us as we'd stepped out into the hallway. I had a sudden feeling as if something terrible was about to happen. I could imagine it all, as if I was in the film I'd seen on the plane, the way it would unfold in a state of unreality that nevertheless insisted upon being negotiated if I didn't want to die. I could feel my heart beating faster but I didn't really know why. We *weren't* in her apartment, even though every one of my senses told me we were. We were in her studio. I went back into the bedroom and walked toward the wall opposite the door, the wall I seemed to have come through when I'd followed S_____ after she'd disappeared. And, just as suddenly as I'd found myself suddenly in S_____'s bedroom, I was back in the empty studio, the locked door out to the hallway in front of me, the faintest hint of sunlight peeking in around the covering on the window. "Okay," I said aloud to myself, and I stepped backwards, trying to isolate the specific moment when my perception shifted, but I couldn't, there was no moment of transition, it simply was the studio and then it was the bedroom wall halfway across the room from where I was standing in the middle of the floor, then I stepped forward again and I was in the middle of the studio, facing the locked door. I looked up at the corners of the room to try to figure out if it was something having to do with mirrors or lights or video projection but I couldn't see anything. I supposed that even if there had been something like that at work I wouldn't have been able to see it even if I'd tried because it would have been obscured by whatever illusion it was casting. Although surely it would be visible in one or the other of the two spaces being—simulated? Was this a simulation? It was more like a simulacrum. Both rooms were real. I stepped back into the bedroom and went over to the bed. My perception didn't shift. I sat on the bed. But then I felt an unnerving sense of impossibility because the bed was further away than the place in the room at which I kept disappearing from the bedroom and moving back to the studio. If this was all the same room, I should have been back in the studio space, not the bedroom. But the bed was absolutely real. The blanket was soft and worn thin in spots. The pillow had a couple hairs on it. There was a cardboard box under the frame. I stood up and began to take slow, tentative steps towards the middle of the wall, towards the area of the room directly beyond where I'd kept moving in and out of the bedroom, and nothing changed, I didn't experience a sudden sense of reorientation, and then just like that I was right in the pathway of whatever I'd thought had been constructed, whatever it was S_____ had managed to pull off. It didn't make sense. If this was the same room, I was now in the doorway to the hall of the building where her studio was. I began to walk forwards, towards the place where I'd kept snapping into the bedroom but now approaching it from behind, approaching it from the same direction I'd been approaching it when walking towards it in the empty studio room, but now I was taking the same steps in the bedroom. It didn't make sense. I kept waiting for S_____ to reappear in the doorway to the apartment hallway, or for something else to happen, to suddenly wind up back in the studio, somehow on the other side of whatever barrier I'd kept passing through, or for something else even less possible to occur. But nothing did. And then I was standing where I'd kept finding myself standing as I'd hit whatever point it was in the room, the studio, that had shifted me into the bedroom, and I was still in the bedroom. I stood there, absolutely still, trying to decide what to do. I looked back over my shoulder. I looked towards the open door to the hallway of the apartment, I looked at my feet, planted firmly on the floor of the bedroom and then, without anything else to do, I looked back up and walked out of the bedroom into the hallway, turned right and went to the door out of the apartment, and I left. And the landing outside the apartment was there. I stumbled on the stairs. I went outside. I took a deep breath on the sidewalk and I turned to look back up at the apartment building. It wasn't the apartment building. It was the studio building. I looked up and down the street but I didn't have any sense of the neighborhood. Everything was unfamiliar. I noticed a bench across the street and I crossed over to it and sat down. It felt good to sit. I let out a deep breath I hadn't realized I'd been holding, the deep breath I'd taken as I'd stepped out of the building, as if a part of me had doubted reality, had felt like stepping out the door was like stepping into space. And of course it was, but not the way I'd involuntarily thought of it. I watched the door of the studio building, waiting to see if S＿＿＿ was going to follow me, but she didn't. Eventually I got back up and went back inside. I climbed the stairs and let myself in.

And I was back in the empty studio space. I closed the door behind me and sat down on the floor just to the side of the door, my back against the wall. I didn't want to do it again. "S____," I said to the empty room, somehow certain that she was right there, on the other side of the invisible barrier between the two rooms, somehow certain that she could somehow see me even though I hadn't been able to see the one room from the other, in either direction, at any point. It was like the feeling of a ghost in a room, or a presence in darkness. I tilted my head back against the wall and closed my eyes. "S____, come back out here," I said, now letting my voice drift up towards the ceiling instead of sending it towards that other room in the same room as me. But she didn't come. I didn't move. Instead, I pulled out my phone, took a photo of the empty room in front of me, then opened the notepad feature by tapping on the little icon made to look like lined notebook paper, and I began to write, tapping the words out with my fingertips, re-correcting the autocorrect mistakes as I went, trying to get my thoughts down while they were still fresh: *whatever it is is a kind of loop, a strange dream. i don't know how it's operating, how it's made, but it puts one in a place of utter disorientation. is it a work of autobiography? the empty studio, the bedroom, the apartment, the bedroom as entry point into the apartment, the studio as invisible background before awakening into the bedroom and then one goes out into the hallway, into the rest of the apartment, into everyday life, adult life, but if one leaves to go out into the world and then tries to get back to where one came from, one is back in the empty studio, the creative place, the blank state, and one starts over again, never arriving, never seeing something created. but is that a commentary on s_____? or on all artistic practice? if the former, will anyone other than someone as close to s_____ as i am even know? what is a portrait of one's home, one's most intimate reality, when gazed upon by someone who doesn't recognize it as such? one invites a misreading.* I typed slowly, pausing at the end of every sentence—after every comma, even—to consider my words, to try to puzzle it out. And when I had finished I looked up and realized, based on the lack of light coming in around the covering on the window, that somehow it had gotten dark outside though not enough time had passed for that to be true. It made no sense but it didn't alarm me, something about it seemed to adhere to a kind of strange logic, as if the strange loop of whatever S_____ had put me through had shunted me into a different relationship to space, to time. S_____ still hadn't reappeared. At some point while writing my notes I had stopped feeling that strange sense of presence, as if she too had gone out through the hallway door of the apartment and not returned. Not come back into the building to join me in the studio. Not come back to me through the strangeness in the bedroom. I put my phone down on the floor, looked around the empty studio one last time, then stood up, opened the door out into the hallway of the building she shared with a handful of other artists, flicked the switch to turn the light off in the studio, and closed the door behind me before heading down the stairs and back outside to return to the apartment building the way we'd come in the morning.

6.

The next morning I woke without any recollection of getting back to the apartment. I went down the hall and paused outside the bedroom door. It was closed. I considered opening it and going in. I wanted to disappear, to reappear. But somehow I knew that wasn't how it would work. And a part of me was scared, I realized, though I wasn't sure what I was scared of. S_____ had never reappeared in the studio. I had no recollection of whether or not I'd seen her later in the evening, back at the apartment when I'd returned at some point. It was like it just slipped away, and now it was morning. I didn't go into the bedroom. I went back down the hall to the kitchen area and made a coffee as I had the day before, but with a strange feeling as if I was repeating myself, trying to re-perform the day before, to conjure S_____, but S____ didn't come down the hall, the door didn't open. I finished making my coffee and went to get my phone from where I'd left it plugged in by the bed in the alcove. I looked at the time. It was much earlier than I'd thought it was. The sunlight was different here. I'd forgotten what it was like. I sat down on the mattress and drank my coffee. I checked to remind myself what time it was back home and decided to call J____ but she didn't answer. A moment later she texted to say that she was on the train heading home from giving a guest lecture to a friend's class at a different university. I texted back to say that was fine, I'd be around, she should text when she got home. I took another sip of my coffee. I was hungry. Had I eaten dinner? Had I eaten anything? Had I really slept? My phone still in my hand, I looked back over my notes from the day before and it was like reading something someone else had written. My legs hurt like I was dehydrated, like I was still on the plane. The quiet of the apartment pressed in on me like the sound of a pressurized cabin. I stood up as if to remind myself that I was on the ground, even if I was a few stories up in the air, nothing was unstable beneath my feet, but then all the blood rushed to my head and I felt dizzy so I sat back down. The feeling persisted. I closed my eyes and breathed slowly and deeply. I felt my body unclench and I took another sip of coffee. Then I heard the bedroom door down the hallway and I looked up, waiting to see S____ appear in the entrance to the alcove, but she didn't appear. I didn't even hear her down the hallway. Had I actually heard the bedroom door? I stood and peered around the edge of the alcove entryway, looking down the hall towards the bedroom. The door was open, though not wide. No one had come out. It wasn't open wide enough for a body to slip through the gap. I set my coffee down and walked down the hall again, but now with a feeling of inevitability, like a body drawn, impelled. I got to the door and pushed it open. I stood still in the doorway and looked in. The room was empty. I looked back over my shoulder to see if I'd simply misperceived the bathroom door as being open even though the bathroom light was off, but no one was there. I was alone. Maybe a strong draft had opened the bedroom door. I stepped into the room and stared at the place in its middle where I knew the studio was hidden out of sight. Nothing made sense… I knew, somehow, that all I would have to do would be to walk to that place and there would be no turning back. Somehow the repeating of the morning and the crossing of that threshold in reverse would cement something into place that I didn't understand but apprehended with absolute clarity, and I considered it for a long while, considered doing it, crossing that threshold, but I couldn't, I couldn't bring myself to do it. It wasn't fear so much as aversion. A kind of magnetic resistance. Instead I turned and left the room, went back down the hall, gathered my things, and left. I walked outside with the single bag I'd brought with me and went downstairs to the sidewalk where I paused to look at my phone for directions to the train station. I'd go visit my parents in New York and come back. S_____ would be back when I returned and we could discuss the work properly, whatever it was. I needed distance to be able to write about it. I needed stability. If the work was the apartment, or included the apartment, then was *I* also the work? And if I was part of the work, how could I write about the work? How could a work of art speak about itself? Even a work of art that included within itself a kind of precis or series of signposts—it wasn't *the work* speaking, it was the artist. But I felt like I had been tricked into coming to write about a work that was separate from me only to discover that the work required my being there—as spectator, as component part, and somehow as voice from within rather than from without—in order to be finished. I had no solid ground. I had no model. I felt queasy as I thought about it, standing outside. I focused on what I was doing and pulled up directions to the train station. What mattered was creating alternative conditions, reclaiming my own status as subject separate from the work in which S_____ had implicated me, in which S_____ had enmeshed me. But could there have been any other way? Would it have worked if she had prepared me? There was no way it would have. Still, to have the beating heart of a work be a sense of betrayal, a kind of invisible labor, and to locate that within the figure of someone intimately connected to the artist and the art, and to site that within a recreation of? or within the actual apartment, the actual home of oneself as the artist? I didn't understand the work itself, or if I did it was a kind of understanding that I didn't want to fully engage with because it was a kind of understanding that looked too much like regarding our relationship through a purely aesthetic lens and finding it to be something made, not grown, something coldly constructed for a particular purpose rather than naturally developed over time. I started walking. The station wasn't too far, no need to catch a cab or deal with the subway or find a bus stop or anything like that. I hadn't packed a heavy bag. I just focused on putting one foot in front of the other. I'd been walking for a few blocks when my phone rang. It was still in my hand. I figured it was J_____ but when I looked at the screen I saw that it was S_____. I stared at the incoming call and felt the phone vibrate in my hand but I didn't answer. After a moment, the call disappeared from my screen, then an automated text message alerted me to the call I'd just missed. I wondered if I'd get another automated message a minute or two later to tell me that I had a voicemail message, or whether S_____ would write a text message, but nothing else came through. I kept my phone in my hand and continued making my way towards the train station. I was halfway there. My phone rang again. This time it was J_____. I must have sounded out of breath when I answered because the first thing she said after I'd said hello was, "Are you running? Is something wrong?" "No," I said, "just walking to the train station." "What for?" "Going to see my parents early. Then I'll come back here before L.A. instead of the other way around." "Is everything okay?" she asked. "Yeah," I said, "I think so. I just need some time to think about the work." "Is it good?" she asked. "I don't know. It's hard to describe," I said, "as a work of art, I mean. I think she built a replica of her entire apartment." "She what?" "Recreated her entire apartment in her studio, or, I don't know, maybe somehow managed to create some sort of pathway from her studio to her apartment? But that doesn't really seem possible, and even if it was, I don't know how it would be something she could transport up to Boston to show." "Like a real replica? To scale and everything?" "Yeah," I said, "except everything was weird." "Have you gotten her to talk about it at all? I feel like that would probably help, right? Even if only to understand what she's trying to achieve? How she's trying to make you feel?" "I haven't, no," I said. I didn't know how or whether to tell her about the door opening, the empty apartment, the lack of my being able to remember coming back from the studio the night before. I kept thinking of sentences I wanted to say to her that I couldn't quite bring myself to say, they got stuck, I felt somehow certain that whatever I had experienced in the last 24 hours wouldn't quite translate, that I wasn't going to be able to make sense, and I wasn't sure I was capable of handling that kind of reaction. I was still managing to reside in a place where aesthetics held everything together, but only barely. I needed to sit with it, to interrogate that place in such a way as to avoid damaging it beyond repair, or if it was going to come down all around me, at least I could hopefully make it a kind of controlled demolition. Instead, I added, "She had to take care of some other stuff today." "You're sure you're okay?" J_____ asked in a way that told me I clearly sounded less balanced than I was trying to sound. Or maybe J_____ and I had just been together for long enough that no amount of trying would make a difference, she knew me too well. "I'm just tired," I said as I spotted the train station up ahead on the next block. "Try to sleep on the train," said J_____. "I will," I said. We said goodbye and I went inside the station to buy a ticket. An hour later I was on a commuter Amtrak headed north to New York. I didn't sleep.

7.

What would it mean if I wrote an exhibition text that failed to explain the work of art? But that didn't seem like the issue I was facing. The issue was that I felt as if explaining it wouldn't do any good. I spent the entire train ride staring out the window, watching the northeast roll past, backs of houses, parking lots, trees covered in tattered remains of plastic bags. It was kind of like sleeping. I listened to the people in the pair of seats behind me talk about what sounded like a movie one of them had seen the night before and that the other person had only heard of in passing. I didn't catch the title. But the person who hadn't seen it, after listening to their companion kind of half-describe it for a minute or two, said, "I'm not going to see it, you should just tell me the whole plot," at which point the person who *had* seen it started properly from the beginning and gave a detailed plot summary of the film, which I almost immediately realized must have been a sequel to the film I'd watched on the plane, or if not a sequel then somehow related to the story of the film I'd seen. The plot summary, as told by the person behind me on the train who had seen the film the night before, started with the main character, the protagonist who had realized he could move through time by stepping in one direction or another, having spent the last year or two training in solitude somewhere remote, on an island in the Pacific, driving into town once a week to get food and water and gas for his generator, driving back to his cabin, sitting incredibly still and trying to focus entirely on the present, then standing slowly and working on taking steps in a way that allowed him to reside in two times at once, whether the present and the past, the present and the future—a kind of step forward that wasn't fully committed to whatever came next—and the present and whatever other presents were just off to one side or the other. This training seemed to take up all of his time, morning till night, and it wasn't at first clear, the person behind me said, why he was so absolutely focused on just this one task, this seeming obsession with these incremental movements, this focus on barely using his power, until the person behind me explained that it became clear, as the opening scenes progressed, how haunted he was by the loss of someone named V_____, which was a name I didn't remember from the film I'd watched, and which made me suspect that probably at least one other film in this series had been made and released between the film I'd seen on the plane and the film that I was listening to a summary of as I sat there on the train, staring out the window. V____ had died, or been lost, in some kind of accident related to the protagonist's power, and the protagonist was death haunted, struggling to come to terms with whatever it meant to have such a power, and trying, too, to figure out how to get V____ back. The person behind me, telling the story, said there was a scene near the end of the opening sequence, after all the training scenes, when the protagonist woke suddenly from a dream in which he and V____ had been together, happily walking along the beach, and he was so certain that what he'd just experienced, just seen, wasn't a dream but was in fact a glimpse of one of the parallel presents he knew were always right there, just a step or two away, that he ran out onto the beach and began to frantically step to the side, to the side again, to the side, and then back to the other side again and again, but always he found himself still alone on the beach, his feet in the water or up at the edge of the dunes, and finally he gave up, dropping to his knees in the surf beneath a cloudless night sky bright with stars and a full moon, and he cried as the scene faded to black and the title of the film came up on the screen. At which point an announcement came on over the train's PA system, saying that the cafe car was open for anyone who wanted to get a cup of coffee or tea or something to snack on during the journey, and the people behind me stopped talking about the film, decided to go see what was on offer, and got up to make their way there. The train car was silent once they'd left. There were other people in various seats around me, but no one else was talking. I kept staring out the window for a while and was considering getting up myself to go walk the length of the train, maybe wind up in the cafe car as well and possibly hear some of the end of the summary of the film, which I assumed had continued once they'd bought whatever they decided to buy and sat down either at one of the little tables in the cafe area or on one of the window-facing benches upstairs in the viewing car, but just as I was about to get up, they came back, holding cardboard hot drinks cups and walking in that slightly measured way that people walk when carrying hot drinks, though the cups had lids on them and were probably already half-empty, based on how long they'd been gone, unless they'd finished their initial drinks and gotten a second one each before coming back. Either way, they came back in through the sliding door that led out to the area between the cars, and were back in their seats behind me before the door had finished sliding all the way shut behind them. "So does it seem like there's going to be a sequel with her as the main character?" the one who hadn't seen the film asked as they were sitting down. The one who had seen the film made a thoughtful sound and didn't answer immediately. Then she said, "It wouldn't surprise me. Her powers would be really cool to see in an entire movie, and there's a little scene halfway through the credits that show her looking in a mirror and seeing a view of her own self from the top down, except it's clearly not the same her who's looking in the mirror, and the bathroom in which the mirror version of her is standing isn't the same as the bathroom in which she herself, seeing the reflection, is standing." "Trippy," said the one who hadn't seen the film. I couldn't remember the name of the original, or rather the one I'd seen on the plane, which was at least 'the original' in my mind, and which certainly had all the hallmarks of a first installment, since it was very much about the character's origins, and I almost wanted to turn around in my seat and ask what the name of the film was, the one they were discussing, since that would be enough for me to search the internet for the name of the one I had seen on the plane but then I decided not to, and instead I tried to find it on the internet simply with broad search terms, plot points, and didn't get anywhere, which wasn't surprising. But I was thinking about the movie by then, and had nothing else to focus on, so I just kind of stared out the window, trying to think more thoughtfully about the film I'd seen on the plane, which felt kind of like a way to trick myself into thinking about whatever it was that I had experienced in S____'s studio, whatever it was she had managed to construct.

My phone was still in my hand and I switched away from the internet browser where I'd been searching for the name of the film and went back again to the notes I'd written the day before while waiting for S_____ to reappear, sitting on the floor of the studio, my back against the wall, or perhaps I hadn't been waiting for her to reappear so much as waiting for the moment when my consciousness would have been able to accept the fact that she wasn't going to reappear. Perhaps all any of it was was a matter of waiting for certain conditions to be met within oneself. I re-read what I'd written and added a couple more sentences about time, which were sentences that seemed to be almost as much about the movie (or movies) as about the studio and the apartment, and then I switched off my phone and got up and went to the cafe car myself, as I'd been about to do earlier, but when I got there the cafe itself was closed, with a sign on the counter saying the cafe attendant would be back in ten minutes, so I went back upstairs to the viewing car and sat down just as we entered a tunnel. The effect of the sudden plunge into darkness was strange and disorienting, the way the effect of first stepping through whatever point existed between the studio and the bedroom had been disorienting, not disorienting in the same way, but in a way that caused me to feel a momentary sense of *déjà vu*, and I lost myself for a moment in my own reflection in the window, but then we came out of the tunnel and I had to blink a few times to clear my vision from the explosion of light that hit my eyes. I looked around the viewing car and then back out the window, now only able to see the faintest hint of my own reflection faintly overlaid onto the landscape on the other side of the glass, the repetitive flow of densely populated suburbs or exurbs, wherever we were. It was the kind of environment I'd grown up in, far enough outside of New York City that I never really went there—to New York City—until I was in my teens, and even then only every once in a while. And then I'd left New York to go study on the west coast and then moved to Australia for work. It was strange when I thought about it, when I considered the random sequence of events that had led me to be someone who had so little attachment to the place I was from. But it wasn't as if I had a particularly deep attachment to the place where I'd lived for basically my entire adult life, either. Maybe it was more accurate to simply describe myself as someone who didn't form particularly deep attachments to place, regardless of circumstance, and that what sometimes seemed like a random sequence of events that had led me to be someone who had so little attachment to the place I was from was actually a random sequence of events that had led me to be someone who simply didn't form deep attachments to place. That made more sense. That felt like a kind of culminating achievement for my parents, who themselves had had complicated relationships to place and home and their own families.

I never felt guilty for not wanting to see them as much as it sometimes felt like I ought to. They never seemed overly interested in making me feel guilty. Visiting them was always a kind of strangely muted experience. They still lived in the home I'd grown up in, but had remodeled it so completely since my childhood that it wasn't really the same home, was barely even the same building. The address was the same. The neighbors were almost all the same. Going back was always simultaneously deeply familiar and utterly alienating. I never looked forward to it, but I didn't dread it. It was something like ambivalence, but less definable, less pronounced. I wasn't sure whether we were still in Maryland or somewhere else. I got up and went back down to the cafe portion of the train car.

8.

I don't know how to write about a work of art while I'm so utterly destabilized—not at home yet on familiar ground. A work of art is meant to destabilize, if successful. Or the kind of art that I find most impactful tends to function that way. But to be destabilized only means anything if one is stable to begin with. I'm just moving from one place to another, places I only half-know anymore, and without J_____. Did I leave Baltimore just so I could go back and hopefully feel a sense of stability upon returning? Or am I hoping to get to New York and feel a sense of some kind of familiarity, even if only tenuous and emotionally complicated? Why did I ignore S_____'s call when I was walking to the train station. Where was she calling from. What if she called now. Would I answer? I could call her back. But does S_____ even matter, if I'm trying to respond to the work? Just got off the phone with J_____ who said she was up late watching the election results come in, waiting to see who the new prime minister will be, that she couldn't get to sleep and just kept reading different news articles on the internet, refreshing her searches, stressing out about whether things would go the way she hoped they would. I asked why she bothered checking on the night of the actual election, when knowing or not knowing wouldn't in any way impact the actual results of the election, wouldn't it make sense to just go to sleep and wake up in the morning to see all the information all at once, after everything was resolved and she could just get the details without the waiting and the anxiety. She said she'd started the day thinking that way, but had been on campus until past dinnertime, working in her office, and the few of her colleagues who were still in their offices had gotten progressively more and more wound up as the evening had come on and results had started to trickle in. She said it had been disconcerting to watch their affects change, the way they had become progressively more and more glued to their phones, occasionally piping up with one bit of information or another, some reported speculation, then lapsing into silence again, and she had left campus still not overly caught up in all of it, if anything she had left campus with a firmer sense of her own lack of interest in the minute-by-minute updates, but then she'd gotten home and instinctively checked one or two things to see how they'd progressed since she'd last heard them mentioned by her colleagues, and then she'd checked again while brushing her teeth and it had just snowballed. There was something kind of invigorating about it. I'd voted in advance by mail. I'd forgotten about it. She told me what it looked like the results were going to be, based on early polling. I asked if she was in bed. She said she was but she was sitting up, that she kept trying to read the book she was trying to finish but kept getting distracted by the news. It just occurred to me, sitting here on the train, nearly to New York now, that S_____ may have created a work of context-specific art. That my being jet-lagged and in a state of semi-familiarity with my environment was a fundamental prerequisite for the work to successfully mean anything. But how can that possibly be a sustainable way of making art? How can that possibly work for more than one or two people as an audience? What if J_____ had come with me? Would that have changed things so completely that maybe S_____ wouldn't have even bothered to take me to the studio? Did she have plans in place, ready to cultivate the necessary conditions in a different way if J_____ and I had shown up together? Did she choose me—was I the first person who popped into her head—because she knew that I, of all her friends, many of whom would have been geographically closer, emotionally closer, etc., that I was the one who was least likely to show up with my partner? If so, then what. What do I do with that, if I decide it's true. Would I have felt any less destabilized if J_____ was with me? I probably wouldn't have stayed with S_____. J_____ and I would have sorted something out so that we had a place of our own. And even if we had come together and wound up staying with S_____, J_____ wouldn't have been alright with just suddenly leaving the way I did this morning. I wouldn't be on *this train right now. The entire sequence of events would have unfolded differently. Earlier, up in the viewing car, I got distracted by my own reflection in the window and kept thinking that I've started to look like my father, but not in the way my father looks the way his father used to. I catch myself acting like my mother but looking like my father. But I only look like my father, at least for now, when I see myself only half-reflected in a dirty train window, and I only seem to be acting like my mother when something is incredibly out of the ordinary. The way I just got up and left S_____'s apartment this morning. I was so unsettled and I just panicked. And then it wasn't until I was on the train that I realized it was just like how she, my mother, always used to just storm out of the house when she was upset and go for walks without even putting on shoes, even when the weather was cold, always when it was just me and her at the house and my father was at work. It used to make me so scared when I was little. That feeling—an absolute certainty that she wasn't coming back. That everything had just changed without my even realizing it was in the process of happening. And I remember the fear that would possess me—at least when I was really little, before I started to figure out ways of coping with it, or had just gotten used to it—when I imagined my father coming home to find me alone and my mother gone, never coming back, and I would have to tell him that she had left, and he would know it had been my fault. But she always came back, always well before he got home. And I never talked about it. I lived in a constant state of reprieve, of feeling like the next time would be the time when* she didn't come back. And then I guess one day I didn't come back, is how it probably felt to her, when I eventually moved out. Or that's how she would probably describe it, being melodramatic. I should call S_____ back. I was being irrational when I ignored her call. I'll call her when I get off the train. The last thing I need is for her to pick up and then for the train to go through a patch where there's bad reception and for the call to drop or get completely mangled, especially if it's right at the start of the call, before I even have a chance to explain where I've gone. We're almost there now anyway. Some things out the window look familiar. What will I say to her if she answers? What if she asks about the work? I don't know what I even experienced. I don't know where the work ended, when it ended. For all I know, I'm still in the work, still am the work, I've been activated and am now in motion until some future point that I'm currently unaware of, and whatever trace I leave throughout the course of that period of activation and motion is what she'll display in Boston. But is that how S_____ works? Will I ask her if that's what's happening? Would she tell me? Why was she calling? Better not to think about all of this. Better not to try to plan it all. There's no way to anticipate all the possibilities. That's why J_____ and I stopped traveling together. I would sour every trip we took by stressing about things we couldn't possibly control. Things that hadn't happened yet. Missed trains. Not enough money. Forgotten documents. And then that stress seeped into everything. We used to fight all the time. Not just on trips. I'll just call when I get off the train. I'll just call and let the conversation happen *however it happens. And I'll go from there. S_____ asked me to come. This is what's eventuated. I have to trust that she's okay with this, or will be. I'll call S_____ and I'll call J_____ and then I'll head to my parents' place. In the meantime, I'll just get another coffee and stare out the window. Sometimes that's all there is to do. I should have brought a book. I suppose I could re-read some of the stuff that S_____ sent me to read on the plane. Maybe it will make more sense now. Maybe all that stuff about trying to make impossible rooms explains everything and all S_____ has done is make an impossible room, just following some obscure methodology outlined in 1975 and never realized until now. I can't stop thinking about that movie I watched on the plane and about the sequel that the people behind me were talking about earlier, before they got off in Philadelphia, as if somehow there's a key to this in that. But every time I almost make a connection between the two, I find myself unable to conclude the idea, like trying to read in a dream. I wish I could just sleep. I don't remember sleeping last night. I remember waking up but not sleeping, not going to sleep. I want to get off this train. I want to get to my parents' place and write whatever I can manage to write about whatever that was that I experienced at S_____'s studio last night and then I want to go back to S_____ and give it to her and then go back home to J_____. I don't like this. The train is slowing down.*

9.

At the train station in New York I went into a convenience store to buy a bottle of water. The woman at the counter, with gray hair cut short, spoke in a kind of disjointed way that made me feel like I was missing every other word. She looked at my fingernails and said something about her children, two boys, both adults now, then told me she had been working since 3:00am and laughed. I didn't know what to say so I didn't say anything and just took my change and left. Afterwards it occurred to me that I could have told her I didn't know what she was talking about. But what good would that have done? Would she have been able to make things any clearer than she already had? Wasn't I the problem? Wasn't the problem that I didn't know? If I went back in, the only thing worth saying would be to apologize for any way in which I may have made her feel ignored or dismissed because of my not understanding what she was talking about. I was tired and jet-lagged and had also just gotten off a train from Baltimore. I wasn't firing on all cylinders. But I didn't go back in. Instead, I sat on a bench in the high ceilinged main hall of the train station and called S_____. It was early evening now. The train station was surprisingly busy. The phone rang a couple times and then went to an answering machine message. I didn't know what to say but I waited for the beep and then just started talking. I said where I was and that I would be back and that I was getting my thoughts together and making notes and that we could talk about the work in a day or two. I said I was sorry for not leaving a note or anything. I started to say something else but then my phone made a noise in my ear and I looked at my screen and saw that she was calling me back, so I awkwardly said something dismissive into the answering machine message I was leaving and hung up the call, switching over to the incoming call from S_____. "Are you there?" I said. "Yeah, where are you?" she asked, a note in her voice that I couldn't quite place. "I was just leaving you a message," I said, before adding, "I'm in New York." "New York?" said S_____ as if she wasn't sure she had heard me right. "I just got to the train station," I said. "What are you talking about?" said S_____. "I woke up this morning," I explained, "and you weren't at the apartment. I freaked out. I'm sorry. The—whatever happened at your studio was—" "I went out for bagels," she said calmly. "What?" I said. "This morning," said S____, "I woke up and you were still sleeping so deeply that you didn't even hear me moving around the kitchen making coffee, so I went out for bagels. And when I came back, you were gone, all your stuff was gone." There was a long silence. "I'm sorry," I said. Another long silence. I wondered if she was about to hang up on me, or whether she'd already hung up. But then she said, "What happened? Why did you leave?" and I can't accurately describe now the swirl of feeling that came over me at that point because it was one of those things that was beyond language. It all happened so instantaneously that to describe it in a way that does justice to the temporality of it would necessarily leave out all of the nuance and complexity, and to do justice to that nuance and complexity would necessarily drag it out for so long that it would make it seem as if the conversation suddenly ground to a halt, which it didn't, at least not for longer than a moment or two, which wasn't any longer than the silence that had preceded her two questions that were really just one question asked two different ways. But what came over me when she broke the silence—a silence that I had been absolutely sure was a silence preceding or communicating the end of the call—was partially a feeling of almost manic relief, insane gratitude, a kind of submission to whatever she might ask of me, no matter how unreasonable, because she hadn't hung up, she hadn't left, but then there was also a feeling of sudden tension, remembering everything I'd been thinking about on the train, trying to decide whether I was artwork or audience or something else, or all of those things at once, so that I heard her words and simultaneously wanted nothing more than to answer her with an almost obscene level of honesty and detail while at the same time I was trying to decide whether she was asking out of concern or a sense of feeling betrayed by my disappearance or because she was trying to monitor my current state, trying to assess the work in progress that I couldn't stop suspecting I'd become, been made into without my knowing it was happening, without my agreeing to any such thing, and I didn't know how to respond to her from both of those places at once, so that when I finally spoke, all I could say was, "I don't know," which was a lie, because I did know, but I didn't know how to say the truth, or I wasn't sure if she *wanted* the truth. I wasn't sure if *I* wanted the truth. So I just said, "I don't know." "Are you coming back?" she asked, because of course she hadn't heard the message I'd been leaving and stopped in the middle of when she called, so I said yes, and told her that I'd be back in a couple days. That I was going to try to get my thoughts in line and write some stuff down. "Other than what you wrote down last night, you mean," she said. I didn't remember saying anything to her about having written anything down. But maybe she'd just guessed or assumed. "Yeah, building on that," I said. "I'll try to find those sketches I was telling you about," she said. "Right," I said automatically. I didn't know what she was talking about. Something in my voice must have sounded off because she asked, in a tone not unlike the tone I'd heard in J_____'s voice when we'd talked in the morning, "You're sure you're okay?" "I'm just tired," I said, feeling like I was re-performing the same conversation with S_____ that I'd had with J_____, wondering if S_____ could tell, could hear the way I was repeating myself, could sense the way my words weren't my own, or were my own but not my own at the same time. The way I had suddenly found myself standing in a space that was both her room and not her room. Had *I* been able to tell? "Did we talk last night?" I asked abruptly, almost involuntarily. The question came into my mind and I asked it. Something about what she'd said, the sketches, the knowing that I'd written—and it *had* been knowing, not guessing or assuming, the way she'd said it had been the way one says something one knows to be true. I couldn't remember anything from the night before. There was a long silence again and I felt my heart rate increasing and a coldness on my forehead, a tingle above my upper lip, something cold and metallic like blood in my mouth, panic, anxiety. "Yeah," she said, sounding suddenly careful. "Right," I said, trying to sound like it had just been a meaningless question, unsure of whether I managed to convince her. She started to say something else but I cut across her—"I need to make my way to my parents' house," I said. "Right," she said, "I guess it's getting late." "For them at least." "I'll try to find those—" she started to say. The sketches. But she didn't finish her thought. Instead she said, "I'll talk to you tomorrow?" "Yeah," I said. Then we hung up and I went to find the bus stop, which wasn't where I remembered it being, and the signage wasn't clear. But it was hours past closing time and the information desk was deserted. I walked around for a little while before finding it. The timetable, its plastic covering covered in scratched graffiti, said the next bus was in twenty minutes. No one else was waiting. I sat down on the bench and leaned my head back against the wall. I was under cover and a slight rain was falling, darkening the sidewalk in front of me, causing the road to glisten under the street lights. I suddenly remembered a line from Moyra Davey's film *Les Goddesses*, which I'd seen at the ICA in Philadelphia last time I'd been in the U.S., years before, about how a narrative moderated by a journey has a special self-generating momentum. "A trip, with its displacements in time and space, can be the perfect way to frame a story." I'd written it down in my notebook at the time, sitting there in the gallery, watching the single channel installation. It had struck me as a good observation at the time, especially as I myself had been on a trip at the time, and it had stayed with me, one of those bits of thought one recalls periodically, though it hadn't popped into my head for a while. I tended to recall it anytime I was unmoored in some way, which wasn't that common an occurrence, or at least wasn't any more common for me than for anyone else I knew. A trip to the hospital to suddenly sit in a waiting area, a flight to another city for a wedding or a funeral, a missed bus or train and then the impulsive decision to get on a different one, believing it to be heading in more or less the right direction and then becoming lost in one's own city, driven down strange roads or getting off at a station that looks familiar but is at the same time completely wrong, uncanny and almost seeming to shimmer slightly if one looked at it too closely. And now in New York, sitting and waiting for the bus—the bus stop no longer where it had been in the past, and still no one else waiting for the bus but me—the Davey line came floating back to me and I wondered, not for the first time, about the other formulations. About using a *story* to frame a *trip*. Or using *displacements in time and space* to frame a trip, or a story. I supposed it all amounted to the same thing. But to the person enmeshed in the formulation, surely the primary operator mattered. Was I on a trip or was I in a story? Was there a difference? Most of Moyra Davey's work took the form of photographs taped into the form of envelopes and mailed to friends of hers in other countries, then unfolded back out once they had arrived at their destinations and displayed on the wall with the tape still on the image as well as the name and address of the person she'd sent it to, along with her own name and address, still written on the image as well, in the rectangular area that had been temporarily made into the face of the 'envelope'. No trip. No displacement. Each work functioning as a dispatch from a specific, defined place. Correspondence—mail art—almost the opposite of travel, of a journey. I heard a sound and looked up to see the bus coming around the corner of the building, its headlights picking out the misty raindrops flicking through the air in its path.

10.

My father was asleep when I got to my parents' house but my mother had stayed awake to let me in. She'd been in the kitchen drinking black tea and doing the crossword in the newspaper. She let me in and then locked the front door behind me, moving around the living room with an over-tired directionlessness that made me feel comparatively steady, as if I'd passed through some kind of gauntlet of exhaustion and arrived on the other side, able to operate according to a different set of rules, at a different register. Or perhaps I was so tired that what seemed to me to be a kind of temporary freneticism in my mother was actually the result of my slow-to-react mind misperceiving what was in fact my mother moving around the living room at a perfectly normal pace, adjusting a couple pillows on the couch, picking something up off the floor, then coming back over to give me a hug. "I missed you," she said, "it's so late, you must be tired." "I am," I said. "Come on upstairs. I made the guest bed for you. Do you want to shower?" "I think so, yeah," I said. I hadn't showered at S_____'s. "I'll get you a towel while you unpack. Is that all you brought?" she asked, gesturing at my small bag. "Yeah," I said, "I'm only in the country for a little while." "Oh, I didn't realize," she said. "Yeah, just a few days," I said. "Have you already been in Baltimore?" she asked. "I was there yesterday, this morning," I said, "and I'm going back but I thought I'd come see the two of you first." We'd been talking in the living room and then on the stairs and then in the upstairs hallway, lowering our voices as we ascended the stairs so that we were whispering at the end so as not to wake my father, asleep in their bedroom just off the landing at the top of the stairs. Their bedroom door was slightly ajar and he had always been a light sleeper. "In here," my mother said, beckoning me towards the door on the other side of the landing, which had been my bedroom door when I was kid and had since been turned into a sewing studio that doubled as a guest room. She opened the door and turned on the light and I was confronted by an explosion of color that almost overwhelmed me as I stepped in and closed the door behind me. It took me a moment to make sense of the room, which was almost completely dominated by what I recognized as a massive loom, having seen them in museums once or twice, in cavernous, institutional rooms where they had always seemed almost proportionate in relation to the space, and always where they had been arranged—composed; not in use as functional objects. This was different. It was made of stained wood, with a bench in front of it and an immense in-progress weaving interlaced onto its warp. The weaving looked random, as if one color after another was being almost indiscriminately brought into play merely as it came to hand, used till it ran out. I couldn't properly comprehend what I was seeing, but a part of me knew that that was because it was still in progress on the loom, and also too close for me to see it all. And I was tired. It was almost too much for my senses to handle. The color seemed to pulse and I got lost in it so that when my mother's voice called me back to my surroundings, I had to blink a couple times to jolt myself enough to look away towards where she was turning back the quilt on the daybed against the wall behind the door we'd come through, adjusting the angle of the lamp on the table next to the pillow. "Turn off the overhead," she said, "see if this is bright enough for you." "When did you get a loom?" I asked. "A couple years ago." "It's huge," I said. "It seems big until you get used to it," she said. I turned off the overhead light and the colors of the weaving-in-progress seemed less intense. The loom seemed more like a shadow now. It was strange to think that this had been my childhood bedroom. It had been vaguely recognizable as such the last time I'd been back to visit. Now it was something else. The walls were a different color. The hardwood floor had been covered with carpet. I couldn't get to the window on the far side of the room even if I wanted to, the loom was too big for me to get around. "Is that light okay?" my mother asked, calling me back to myself. It was dim but not too dim. "Yeah," I said, "thanks." "I'll see you in the morning," she said, pausing in the doorway to add, "Your father's been waking up early to work on a sculpture in the garden. I never hear him but it might wake you up." "What kind of sculpture?" I asked. My father had been a machinist all his working life and finally retired in the last couple years; my mother had mentioned in emails that he'd started building things in the backyard but I'd never bothered to ask about them, it seemed pointless to ask her to describe something that probably needed to be seen if it stood any chance of being comprehended. But I asked now without even really thinking about it. Something about being reminded that whatever my father had been working on recently—as well as whatever else he'd spent time working on for the last couple years—was just beyond the back wall of the room I was in, outside in the dark beneath the misty rain I'd been sitting in only an hour or so ago, outside the train station. Even though asking now was functionally no different than asking in an email, I didn't retract the question or follow it with something else to change the subject, didn't just say goodnight. "Oh," my mother said, seeming almost caught off guard by my question, "it's kind of a structure—you go into it." "How long has he been working on it?" "Just since last month," she said. I turned back towards the loom and considered asking about the weaving, the same questions, but the questions I had weren't the same, and they weren't questions I knew how to ask. I wasn't even sure they were questions. It was different when something was in the room with you. "Goodnight," my mother said, and she closed the door behind her as she left the room. A moment later I heard the door to the upstairs bathroom close, and a little while later I heard the toilet flush and the sink turn on, then the bathroom door opening again, then the door to my parents' bedroom closing. The sounds were all so familiar—the intervals between each one, even—as to feel almost synced to my body's own rhythm and timbre, as if I was inhaling and exhaling in time to the sounds as they occurred, as I anticipated each one coming. Then the house was silent. I wanted to get around the loom to the window to look outside and see if it was still raining, just to settle myself into the room the way one sometimes needs to map the outer edges of a space before one can relax within it. Instead I opened my bag and got out my toothbrush and toothpaste, along with some clean underwear. I'd go downstairs to shower. The upstairs bathroom's shower was just on the other side of the wall from my parents' bedroom. Showering at night felt loud, disruptive. I opened the bedroom door carefully so as not to creak it on its hinges, then went downstairs in the dark, making my way by memory to the kitchen where I turned on the lights and continued through to the downstairs bathroom. I closed the door and turned the shower on to let it warm up as I undressed. The noise of the running water was loud and comforting. The bathroom was small and filled with steam almost immediately. I left the exhaust fan off. It was like being in a sauna. I stepped into the shower and let the water prickle my skin until I'd adjusted to the temperature, then I washed myself and turned off the water. I stood there in the shower with the door closed for a moment longer, letting the steam rise off my skin, then I got out and dried off, got dressed, went back out into the kitchen. I boiled the kettle to make myself a cup of tea. I didn't just want to fall asleep even though I was tired. I wanted to pause in a way I didn't feel like I had since getting off the plane—that had been two nights ago. My parents' electric kettle took a long time to come to a boil with the weaker American current. As the sound of the agitated water slowly rose in volume, the rumble building towards a boil, I heard a different sound, something irregular but consistent that seemed to be coming from outside on the street, a thud like something heavy but breakable being thrown into a dumpster, then a pause, then the sound again. I heard it a few times before getting up from the chair I'd sunk onto while I waited for the kettle. I left the kitchen and moved the length of the house to look out the front window. The sound came again, sounding no different from nearer the front of the house than it had from the kitchen, when it had been partially masked by the sound of the kettle coming to a boil. But this time, after that initial sound which I'd heard from the kitchen, there was another sound, a kind of hissing slide that changed in pitch once or twice before suddenly being cut short by the same loud sound again. I got to the window just in time to see a single skateboarder out on the street, just at the entrance to the empty parking lot across from my parents' house, the skateboarder coming down hard on the front of his board and not managing to land whatever move he'd been trying to do, the banging sound coming from his board hitting the pavement. He used the toe of his sneaker to flip the board back into position then stepped onto it with enough confidence that it was clear that he at least knew how to ride, if not make the board leave the ground and come back down the way he wanted it to. The hissing sound of his wheels on the concrete as he rolled around in a curve back towards the middle of the parking lot, pushing with his foot once or twice to build up a bit of speed before trying to pop his board up again, and again coming down wrong, stumbling. The sound echoed off the surrounding houses. I stood still in the window, vaguely aware of the silence from the kitchen where the kettle had come to a boil and automatically turned off. I'd go back to it in a moment. I wondered how long it would be until someone in one of the houses around the parking lot, maybe even one of my parents, went out to tell him to leave, or yelled out from a window, or called the cops. He pushed into a graceful curve again, rolling for a little longer this time. I could see that he had earbuds in. He pushed once more then bent his knees slightly, crouching his body into position on the board before suddenly uncoiling. He landed it this time. The sound was similar but less harsh as he came back down. He continued to roll along, then brought himself back around in a smooth curve and left the parking lot, rolling into the middle of the street and disappearing down the block. I went back to the kitchen and made a cup of tea.

11.

S____ didn't care what I was doing. I woke up in the morning and stared at the loom from the daybed without moving. The sunlight coming in through the window behind it lit up the weaving like stained glass. Outside, in the yard, I could hear the sounds of tools being used. I got up and could see, now that the room was lit differently—no longer illuminated by artificial light the way it had been the night before—that I could in fact get around the other side of the loom and to the back in order to see out the window. I edged around and got over so I could see down into the yard. My father was out there in jeans and a flannel shirt hammering what looked like scrap metal that was up on some sawhorses. Next to him was a tall sort of triangular structure made of dented, shaped metal that came all the way down to the ground in places and in other places jutted out, its edges sharp-looking, the overall form of the thing not yet suggesting completion or balance. He stopped hammering for a moment, re-positioned the metal, then started hammering again. I moved away from the window and left the room to go downstairs. My mother wasn't around, as far as I could tell. There was coffee in the coffeepot. I wasn't sure whether I felt like going outside to talk to my father but why else was I even here other than to see them, my parents. I went to the front door to get my shoes, brought them back to the kitchen and pulled them on before stepping outside. The air was cool. I shoved my hands down into my pockets as I crossed the patio to where my father was working. He had his back to me so I called out to get his attention, not wanting to startle him. He stopped hammering and straightened up before turning to face me. I recalled my reflection in the window of the train. "Your mother said you might sleep late," he said. Somehow I hadn't noticed the time. "What time is it?" "Past noon." That seemed impossible and I looked up at the sky but the sun was completely hidden by clouds. "Why didn't either of you wake me up?" I asked. "I figured all my banging around would do the trick," he said. "How long have you been working out here?" "I took a break for a cup of coffee a couple hours ago. But I started right after breakfast." "It doesn't bother the neighbors?" "They're all deaf from living so close to the highway," he said. "Did you hear that skateboarder last night?" I asked. "Not that I remember," said my father, "I'm probably mostly deaf too." "I don't think you're *deaf*," I said, "maybe just good at tuning stuff out." "Yeah, maybe so," he said, before gesturing towards the house and saying, "Anyway, I was just about to have lunch. Want to join me?" "Sure," I said. We went into the kitchen. I sat down at the table as he went to the fridge and began to pull out various containers of leftovers. He arrayed them on the counter and pulled out a couple of plates which he began to fill almost indiscriminately, arranging portions of different dishes alongside one another the way a painter might prepare colors on a board or palette before starting to work. He got our plates full then grabbed a couple forks and set everything on the table. "Want a beer?" he asked. It felt like morning. I'd just woken up. "No thanks," I said. He seemed to pause then, clearly wondering whether he should still have one himself, and I almost started to say something, to grant him permission, but then he went to the fridge and got one before joining me at the table. "Your mother's out buying thread," he said, "for the loom." He took a long drink of beer. "What are you making out there?" I asked. He took a bite of food, chewed it, swallowed, then said, "A camera obscura." "Excuse me?" I said. "A camera obscura," he said again, "like a pinhole camera." "I'm familiar with the concept. I just wasn't sure I'd heard you right," I said. "I thought it would be interesting," he said with a shrug. I took a bite too and we both chewed in silence. He had another long drink of beer. "Your mother said you're going to head back down to Baltimore again?" he said, phrasing it as a question. "Yeah, I'm not done there. But I wanted to make sure I got up here for a visit." "We could have come down and met you there," he said. "Yeah, but I figured this would be easier. Besides, I wouldn't have had anywhere for you to stay." "We would've sorted something out." "I don't mind coming up." "Alright," he said. "What made you want to build a camera obscura?" I asked. He shrugged the same way he'd shrugged a moment ago and said again, "Seemed like an interesting project." "Have you ever been inside of one before?" I asked. He shook his head. "No," he said, "I've seen some pictures and read some books to get a sense of what to do. It's pretty straightforward." "Can I look inside after we eat?" I asked. "Sure," he said, "it's not done but it's coming along." "How much longer do you think you have until you finish?" I asked. "Maybe another year or so. I'm slow. I'm not trying to win any awards." "Do you know what mom's working on?" I asked. "Upstairs?" he said. I nodded. "I think it's an annunciation scene," he said. "Really?" "I think so, yeah. But maybe she changed her mind." "I wanted to ask her last night but I was so tired and she seemed pretty out of it too." "She hasn't been sleeping very well. She watches the news and gets all wound up." "There's a lot to get wound up about," I said. "Yeah, that's true. But I tell her she shouldn't watch it before bed. It doesn't do any good." "What do you do?" I asked. "What do you mean?" "What do you do before bed instead of watching the news? While she's watching the news?" "Read books about camera obscuras, mostly. Right now, at least." "Like manuals about how to make them?" "Yeah, and historical stuff. I buy it all off the internet." "Do you dream about them? About the project?" "I don't dream," he said. Just then the front door opened, we could hear it from the kitchen, and my mother's voice came from the front of the house. "Home!" she called. It was a habit she'd always had, announcing herself to anyone who might be within earshot. Maybe she figured my father would be inside by now, since it was right around lunchtime. "Hi," I said, loud enough for my voice to carry out through the kitchen doorway and to the front of the house. "Oh good—you're up," she said, her voice coming nearer as she spoke. She appeared in the kitchen doorway holding a brown paper bag, which she held up, saying, "Thread." "We're just finishing lunch," said my father. "When did you get up?" my mother asked me. "Just a little while ago," I said. "I thought you might need to sleep," she said. "Did you hear a skateboarder last night?" my father asked her. "I heard something," she said, "but it only sort of woke me up so I wasn't sure if I'd been dreaming or not. Why?" "Apparently someone was out front of the house skateboarding last night," said my father. "Oh. Well, it didn't really bother me." "Yeah, I didn't hear a thing," said my father, "but you know how I am." My mother rolled her eyes and said, "Yeah, only a light sleeper when it comes to anyone in your actual family moving around inside the house, but set off a pipe bomb out on the street and you'd wake up in the morning fresh as a daisy." My mother set the paper bag of thread on the counter and opened the cabinet to get a plate. She served herself some leftovers and joined us at the table. "Sorry there's nothing fancy," she said to me. "This is fine," I said. "I actually need to go grocery shopping, I could've gone while I was out just now but the place where I buy thread is in the opposite direction, it would have been a lot of driving." "It's fine," I said. She ate a couple bites and then stood up to get the salt shaker. She came back to the table and salted her food absentmindedly, staring past me at the dishwasher as if temporarily in a slight trance. "Think I'll head back out," my father said, pushing his chair back and standing to take his plate to the sink, "keep working." "Is it going well?" my mother asked. "As well as can be expected." "Did you go out to have a look?" she asked me. I nodded and said, "I went out when I woke up but I was going to go back out in a bit to take a look inside." "I'll get that new piece attached right now," my father said. "Don't hurt your back again," my mother said to him. "I'll use the lifting thing," he said. Then he left. A minute or so later the hammering started up again from the backyard. After we'd been sitting in silence for a minute or two longer, I said to my mother, "I asked dad if he knew what you're working on upstairs and he said he thought it was an—" "Annunciation," she said, "did he say annunciation?" "Yeah," I said. She nodded. "He kept getting it wrong and calling it an Ascension. We had a big fight about it," she said. "Well he got it right," I confirmed. "Good," she said, "finally." She finished the last bite or two that had still been on her plate. As she chewed I asked, "What made you want to do an Annunciation?" She looked at me as if the thought had never crossed her mind, to consider *why*, then she said, "I don't really know. I just started weaving and at first I wasn't weaving anything in particular and then I just realized that what I was weaving was an Annunciation." "You mean you realized you'd been weaving a scene without meaning to?" "No, there's no scene," she said, as if that should have been obvious already, "it's just that at first I was weaving something that didn't really have a sense of direction or purpose and then suddenly I realized that there *was* direction, there *was* purpose." "Right," I said. "Did you feel it?" she asked. "Like, touch it?" I said. "No—the energy from it. In the room last night." I shook my head and said, "I didn't feel anything." "You were tired," she responded, as if that explained something.

12.

Back outside, my father was on a ladder next to the camera obscura—he'd used some clamps to attach and hold in place the sheet of metal that he'd been hammering. He had a welding mask pulled up and the welding torch in his right hand, holding on to the ladder with his left. "Stand back for a second," he said to me. I stood by the back door while he pulled the mask down and worked. I was barefoot inside my sneakers and the shoe material felt cold against my skin. My shoes felt too big on my feet without my socks on. "Okay," he said, climbing down the ladder and pulling the welding mask off entirely, setting it down on top of one of the sawhorses he'd had the metal on when I'd come out before lunch, "come on over." I crossed the yard and bent down to peer in under one of the raised, open portions of the structure's wall.

The inside was dim but not fully dark yet. My father came up behind me and bent down too. "Step inside," he said, "you can stand up in there." I stoop-walked in and tentatively straightened up once I'd gotten to the middle of the enclosed area. My father came in after me. From inside, the sound of the highway and any birds and whatever else there was in the yard and out on the street and in the neighbors' yards, it was all barely audible. It seemed even less dark inside, too, now that I wasn't peering in from a sunlit exterior. "I'll be closing it up the rest of the way soon," he said, "so the only light that gets in will be through the pinhole." "Where's the hole?" I asked, turning to look around at the walls and not seeing any prick of light coming through. I wondered if maybe my eyes just weren't able to see what was probably a very small light because the interior wasn't yet dark enough, my eyes were too over-saturated. "Up there," he said, pointing up. I looked to where he was pointing and saw a tiny point of light in the center of the domed ceiling. "I thought they tended to be built to project something against one wall," I said. "Usually, yeah," he said, "but not always." "So it will project clouds against the floor?" "Clouds, empty sky, birds, airplanes." I looked back down at the ground beneath my feet, trying to imagine a projection of the sky, but something occurred to me just as I managed to conjure the image up in my mind. "Won't it project onto whoever is standing in here, though?" I asked. "Only if you stand in the middle the way we are right now. Once it's finished it will be the kind of thing where you come inside and want to stay at the edge." "Like at the edge of a pond," I said quietly. I stepped back almost automatically to where I imagined I would position myself if the space was dark and the pinhole in the ceiling was projecting the outside world onto the ground in front of me. The interior of the structure wasn't as small as I'd imagined it would be while I'd been standing outside of it. My father mirrored my movements, stepping towards the other edge and then extending his left leg about two feet in front of him towards the middle point where we'd been standing, marking a spot on the ground with the toe of his sneaker. "Right about here should be the edge of the projected image," he said, "if I did my math right." "Too bad it's not finished," I said. "Stay here," said my father, and he stooped and ducked out through one of the openings in the wall. I looked back up at the ceiling and tried to discern any change in the quality of the light coming through the minuscule hole, a flickering, a brightening or dimming, the sun going or coming out from behind a cloud, but it was almost completely unwavering. I looked back levelly across the space towards the place in the wall through which my father had gone. I could hear myself breathing—a steady, level sound. "Am I waiting for something?" I said aloud, projecting my voice so he'd hear me even if he'd gone to the other side of the yard, but there was no response. My voice didn't resonate the way I had expected it to when I raised it. It sounded hollow and flat, as if the walls were made from something more sound-dampening than metal, and as if the structure's curved wall wasn't only partially finished, with plenty of openings in it. I supposed the openings prevented the sound from reverberating, and the degree to which the space was at least *mostly* enclosed accounted for the flattening of sound, but it was still an unexpected effect. I was about to duck out through the opening that I was closest to when suddenly the entire space went completely black as if a switch had been flipped. I spun around involuntarily, an animal part of me reacting as if there was an immediate threat, but I couldn't see anything. I reached out my hand and felt the cool metal of the wall and somehow that seemed to calm me, as if all I'd needed was some kind of primitive reassurance that the world was still there. I could still feel the ground under my feet. And after a moment or two I realized it wasn't completely dark, just incredibly dim. I turned back around and saw that the space had been transformed. Passing down from the ceiling was a thin column of light, or perhaps it wasn't so much a column as a line of light, less as if it possessed a physicality than as if it was drawn through the space, like a mark on a piece of paper. I only noticed it because of the faint movement of dust particles drifting through it. And below that movement— mirroring it, in a way—was the subtle movement of the projected image, ending almost at exactly the spot on the ground where my father had indicated it would. There was a single cloud drifting across the patch of sky that was visible at my feet. After a moment it was no longer there and the patch of sky was just light, unchanging. Another moment later a different cloud drifted into view, so slowly as to almost seem, from the moment it appeared, as if it had been there all along. I watched it with an almost transfixed sense of fascination, focusing on it more closely than I could ever remember having focused on the movement of a single cloud before. After some period of time had passed, the cloud was filling the projected image so completely that it was no different than it had been before, when the image had been of a sky with no clouds at all; it was just a circle of light. And then the cloud continued to pass out of the image, its edge appearing now at the same edge where it had first appeared. The way the movement was framed made it start to feel less like lateral movement and more like something unfolding in a kind of circular ebb. I took a step to my left and then returned to my original position, as if testing the space, testing my perception from a slightly different vantage point. I did the same to the right, a single step then a return to my initial position. By the time I had finished this careful shifting back and forth, from one side to the other and back again, the large cloud that had temporarily filled the entire image had disappeared completely. Nothing else had come to replace it. I couldn't tell how long it had been. The low light and the muted quality of the sound, the movement of the dust and the projected image—it was a strange effect. I kept almost having thoughts but then never articulating them to myself, as if none of them were worth thinking. I'd never slowed down enough to notice the shape of a thought, like the shape of a cloud, or the shape of the sky right after a cloud had passed across it, a negative shape or a shape within a shape. A thought noticed but not thought. It wasn't right to call such a thing a thought. It was the projected image of a thought. The mind a dark space through which images passed briefly before disappearing again into nothingness beyond the edge of the frame. I closed my eyes to shut out the projection on the floor for a moment, and almost as soon as I'd done so, I could hear sounds from outside of the structure again, they'd been there the whole time, I'd been hearing them but not realizing it. The same sounds of the highway, of birds, of a lawnmower and the beeping of a truck backing up somewhere far enough away that it was only faint but still audible, my father shifting things around—tools, materials—clearly trying to be quiet, the way someone moves carefully around a sleeper, moves with a kind of reverence, a self-aware kind of moving, each movement only what can't be turned into a deliberate non-movement. I opened my eyes again but continued to focus on the sounds from outside. The projected image was still there but it didn't overwhelm me this time. I stared at it for a moment or two longer, then turned around and ducked down towards where I remembered the opening was that I'd come through to get in. My fingers touched the cool, yielding material of a plastic tarp. I pushed against it until a crack of blinding sunlight appeared down low, where the tarp met the ground. I pushed a little more to widen the crack and let my eyes adjust, then I lifted the tarp the rest of the way and stoop-walked out. It felt like I'd been in there for hours. I looked around for my father but couldn't see him anywhere. After a moment or two, however, I heard a sound from the other side of the structure and went around to where the sound had come from. He was affixing clamps to another piece of metal that he'd clearly just gotten into place. He'd lifted the tarp up to get at the unfinished section he was working on. I hadn't heard him moving any of it, though—the metal, the tarp, cutting or shaping the metal if he'd had to. I wondered if he'd been waiting for me to come out before he did anything that would make too much noise or would let light into the interior. He didn't look like he'd been idly waiting. "Need a hand?" I asked him. "Sure," he said, "hold these here while I get the bottom corners secured." I did as he said. We worked without talking much more for another hour or so then I went inside to get a drink of water.

EXHIBITION TEXT
by D. Frederick Thomas

Invited by a formerly estranged friend to write about
her enigmatic new artwork for an upcoming show, an
unnamed narrator makes the journey from Brisbane to
Baltimore hoping to make sense of things both past and
present. Following the strange logic of a Möbius strip,
Thomas's debut grapples with the question of how to
move through the world when one's sense of self is
suddenly and fundamentally fractured. Recalling the
early work of poet-novelist Paul Auster, and coupled
with rare vulnerability, humour and great charm,
Exhibition Text is a deeply layered investigation into
the nature of self, reality, art and perception. Thomas
magically balances contemporary anxiety and a deep
existential curiosity to conjure moments of radiant
insight and a profound, very human beauty in a debut
that will quickly establish Thomas as a unique and
essential voice among the emerging generation of
Australian writers of experimental fiction.

About the author

Originally from Philadelphia, D. Frederick Thomas is
a Brisbane-based Australian writer and artist whose
work has appeared in publications such as Fence, Heavy
Feather Review and Island. In 2023, Thomas's collection
Work Poems was shortlisted for the Arts Queensland
Thomas Shapcott Poetry Prize.